To Will,

From

Grandma

Christmas 2010

A MINEDITION BOOK

PUBLISHED BY PENGUIN YOUNG READERS GROUP

TEXT COPYRIGHT © 1999 BY PAUL AUSTER
ABRIDGED FROM THE ORIGINAL NOVEL,
PUBLISHED IN 1999 BY HENRY HOLT AND COMPANY, INC.
ILLUSTRATIONS COPYRIGHT © 2008 BY JULIA GOSCHKE
ORIGINAL TITLE: TIMBUKTU
COPRODUCTION WITH MICHAEL NEUGEBAUER PUBLISHING LTD., HONG KONG.
RIGHTS ARRANGED WITH "MINEDITION" RIGHTS AND LICENSING AG, ZURICH, SWITZERLAND.
PUBLISHED SIMULTANEOUSLY IN CANADA.
MANUFACTURED IN CHINA BY WIDE WORLD LTD.
TYPESETTING IN "MISPRINTED TYPE"
COLOR SEPARATION BY JULIA GOSCHKE.

LIBRARY OF CONGRESS CATALOGING-IN-PUBLICATION DATA AVAILABLE UPON REQUEST.

ISBN 978-0-698-40090-0
10 9 8 7 6 5 4 3 2 1
FIRST IMPRESSION

FOR MORE INFORMATION PLEASE VISIT OUR WEBSITE: WWW.MINEDITION.COM

Paul Auster

TIMBUKTU

Adapted and illustrated by

Julia Goschke

MR. BONES KNEW THAT WILLY WASN'T LONG FOR THIS WORLD. THE COUGH HAD BEEN INSIDE HIM FOR OVER SIX MONTHS, AND BY NOW THERE WASN'T A CHANCE IN HELL THAT HE WOULD EVER GET RID OF IT.

WHAT WAS A POOR DOG TO DO? MR. BONES HAD BEEN WITH WILLY SINCE HIS EARLIEST DAYS AS A PUP, AND BY NOW IT WAS NEXT TO IMPOSSIBLE FOR HIM TO IMAGINE A WORLD THAT DID NOT HAVE HIS MASTER IN IT. EVERY THOUGHT, EVERY MEMORY EVERY PARTICLE OF THE EARTH AND AIR WAS SATURATED WITH WILLY'S PRESENCE.

THERE WAS NO TIME TO MAKE A FULL INVENTORY, FOR NO SOONER DID THE MEN GET OUT OF THE CAR THAN ONE OF THEM STARTED TALKING TO WILLY

"CAN'T STAY THERE, PAL. YOU GOING TO MOVE ON OR WHAT?"

AND AT THAT MOMENT WILLY TURNED, LOOKED STRAIGHT INTO HIS FRIEND'S EYES, AND SAID,

"BEAT IT, BONESY. DON'T LET THEM CATCH YOU,"

AND BECAUSE MR. BONES KNEW THAT THIS WAS IT, THAT THE DREADED MOMENT WAS SUDDENLY UPON THEM, HE LICKED WILLY'S FACE, WHIMPERED A BRIEF FAREWELL AS HIS MASTER PATTED HIS HEAD FOR THE LAST TIME, AND THEN TOOK OFF, CHARGING DOWN NORTH AMITY STREET AS FAST AS HIS LEGS COULD TAKE HIM.

AS MR. BONES TROTTED ALONG THE SIDEWALK, LISTENING TO A SIREN APPROACH THE AREA HE HAD JUST LEFT, HE UNDERSTOOD THAT THE LAST PART OF THE STORY WAS ABOUT TO BEGIN. HE WAS ON HIS OWN, AND LIKE IT OR NOT, HE WOULD HAVE TO KEEP ON MOVING, EVEN IF HE HAD NOWHERE TO GO.

HE HAD DISGRACED HIMSELF, AND EVEN THOUGH HE TRIED NOT TO DWELL ON WHAT HAD HAPPENED, HE COULDN'T ESCAPE THE FEELING THAT HE WAS OLD

AND WASHED UP, A HAS-BEEN.

IF HE COULDN'T DEPEND ON PEOPLE FOR HIS FOOD ANYMORE, WHAT CHOICE DID HE HAVE BUT TO DEPEND ON HIMSELF?

IT WAS AS IF EVERYTHING HAD SUDDENLY GONE DARK,
AS IF AN ECLIPSE WERE
TAKING PLACE INSIDE HIS SOUL
AND WHILE IT WAS NEVER CLEAR
TO HIM EXACTLY HOW HE KNEW IT,
HE WAS CERTAIN THAT THE MOMENT HAD
COME FOR WILLY TO LEAVE THIS WORLD.

BAD AS THE DAY HAD BEEN, THE NIGHT WAS EVEN WORSE,
FOR THIS WAS THE FIRST NIGHT HE HAD EVER SPENT ALONE, AND
WILLY'S ABSENCE WAS SO STRONG, SO PALPABLE IN THE AIR AROUND HIM.

THIS KID MEANT HIM NO HARM,
AND IF MR. BONES WAS WRONG
ABOUT THAT, THEN HE WOULD
TURN IN HIS DOG BADGE AND
SPEND THE REST OF HIS LIFE
AS A PORCUPINE.

FOR MR. BONES, HENRY PROVED THAT LOVE
WAS NOT A QUANTIFIABLE SUBSTANCE. THERE WAS
ALWAYS MORE OF IT SOMEWHERE, AND EVEN AFTER
ONE LOVE HAD BEEN LOST, IT WAS BY NO MEANS
IMPOSSIBLE TO FIND ANOTHER.

IF HENRY'S FATHER CAUGHT SO MUCH AS A WHIFF OF THE DOG ANYWHERE IN THE NEIGHBORHOOD, THE BOY WOULD BE PUNISHED SO SEVERELY THAT HE WOULD WISH HE HAD NEVER BEEN BORN.

GIVEN THAT MR. CHOW BOTH LIVED AND WORKED IN THE SAME BUILDING, IT SEEMED ALMOST PREPOSTEROUS FOR THEM TO THINK THEY COULD AVOID DISCOVERY.

HE HAD NO IDEA WHERE HE WAS GOING, BUT HE KNEW THAT HE COULDN'T STOP, THAT HE HAD TO KEEP ON RUNNING UNTIL HIS LEGS GAVE OUT ON HIM OR HIS HEART EXPLODED IN HIS CHEST.

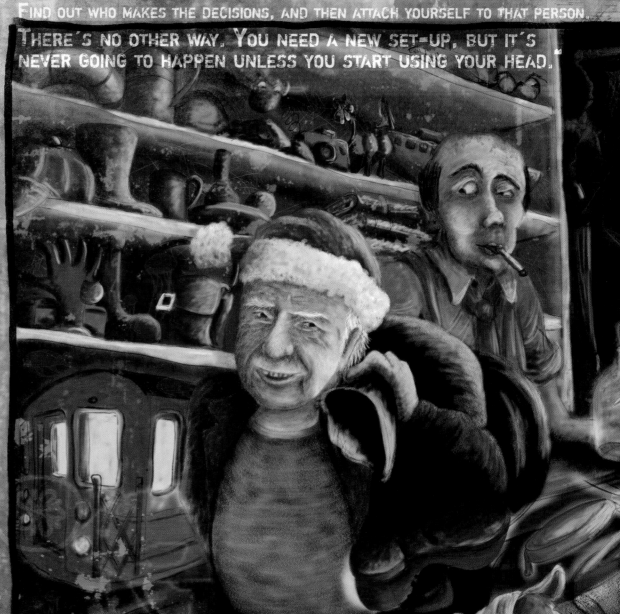

"YOU HAVE TO GO STRAIGHT TO THE TOP, MR. BONES.
FIND OUT WHO MAKES THE DECISIONS, AND THEN ATTACH YOURSELF TO THAT PERSON.
THERE'S NO OTHER WAY. YOU NEED A NEW SET-UP, BUT IT'S
NEVER GOING TO HAPPEN UNLESS YOU START USING YOUR HEAD."

IT WAS THE
FIRST TIME

SINCE HIS MASTER'S DEATH THAT HE HAD BEEN ABLE
TO THINK ABOUT SUCH THINGS WITHOUT FEELING CRUSHED BY SORROW,
THE FIRST TIME HE HAD UNDERSTOOD THAT MEMORY WAS A PLACE,
A REAL PLACE THAT ONE COULD VISIT, AND THAT TO SPEND A FEW MOMENTS
AMONG THE DEAD WAS NOT NECESSARILY BAD FOR YOU, THAT IT COULD IN
FACT BE A SOURCE OF GREAT COMFORT AND HAPPINESS.

"DON'T GIVE UP
ON MEN, BONESY.
YOU'VE HAD SOME HARD
KNOCKS, BUT YOU'VE GOT
TO TOUGH IT OUT AND
GIVE IT ANOTHER TRY."

HE KNEW THAT WILLY
HADN'T REALLY BEEN THERE
WITH HIM ON THE SUBWAY,
AND HE KNEW THAT HE
COULDN'T REALLY TALK,

BUT

IN THE AFTERGLOW OF HIS DREAM
ABOUT IMPOSSIBLE AND BEAUTIFUL THINGS,
HE SENSED THAT WILLY WAS STILL WITH HIM.
IT WAS AS IF HE WERE WATCHING HIM, AND
EVEN IF THE EYES THAT LOOKED DOWN ON
HIM WERE ACTUALLY INSIDE HIM,
IT MADE NO DIFFERENCE IN THE LARGER
SCHEME OF THINGS, BECAUSE

THOSE EYES WERE
THE EXACT DIFFERENCE BETWEEN
FEELING ALONE IN THE WORLD
AND NOT FEELING ALONE.

WARY OF ADVANCING ANY FARTHER,
MR. BONES REMAINED WHERE HE WAS,
WATCHING THE SCENE FROM HIS LITTLE
HIDEOUT AT THE VERGE OF THE WOODS.
HE HAD NO WAY OF
KNOWING IF THIS FAMILY WAS
PRO-DOG OR ANTI-DOG,
NO WAY OF KNOWING IF THEY
WOULD TREAT HIM WITH
KINDNESS OR CHASE
HIM FROM THEIR PROPERTY.

BEFORE HE COULD MAKE UP HIS MIND ABOUT
WHAT TO DO NEXT, THE DECISION WAS TAKEN
OUT OF HIS HANDS.

Before they could break out the champagne, however, Dick butted in with a few additional points — the fine print, so to speak. It's not that he didn't want everyone to be happy, he said, but for the time being it had to be understood that they were only keeping the dog on a "trial basis," and unless certain conditions were met — and here he gave Alice a long, hard look — the deal was off.

WHEN DICK WAS AROUND,
MR. BONES WOULD BE CONFINED
TO THE OUTDOORS, BUT WHEN DICK
WAS GONE, SHE WAS IN CHARGE,
AND THAT MEANT THAT DOGS WERE
ALLOWED IN THE HOUSE.

IT WAS A SUBLIME
VINDICATION TO BE
TOOLING DOWN THE
ROAD LIKE THAT, WITH THE
MAGNIFICENT POLLY AT THE
WHEEL OF THE PLYMOUTH VOYAGER
AND THE MOTION OF THE VAN RUMBLING
INSIDE HIS MUSCLES AND HIS NOSE
TWITCHING CRAZILY AT EACH PASSING SMELL.

WHEN THEY FINISHED WITH HIM AN HOUR
AND A HALF LATER, HE EMERGED AS AN
ALTOGETHER DIFFERENT DOG.
GONE WERE THE SHAGGY CLUMPS OF FUR DANGLING
FROM HIS HOCKS, THE MESSY PROTRUSIONS JUTTING
FROM HIS WITHERS, THE HAIR HANGING IN HIS EYES.

INDOLENCE WAS THE ONLY CHORE ON THE AGENDA,
BUT DICK KEPT MENTIONING WHAT A BIG DAY IT WAS,
KEPT HARPENING ON HOW
"THE MOMENT OF TRUTH HAD FINALLY COME,"
AND AFTER A WHILE MR. BONES BEGAN TO WONDER
IF HE HADN'T MISSED SOMETHING. HE HAD NO IDEA WHAT
DICK WAS TALKING ABOUT, BUT AFTER ALL THESE MYSTERIOUS
PRONOUNCEMENTS, IT DIDN'T SURPRISE HIM THAT ONCE POLLY
RETURNED FROM DROPPING OFF TIGER, HE WAS ASKED TO
JUMP INTO THE VAN AND TAKE ANOTHER RIDE.

IN DUE TIME, HE EXPLORED THE DAMAGE
AND DISCOVERED WHAT WAS MISSING, BUT BECAUSE
HE WAS A DOG AND NOT A BIOLOGIST OR A
PROFESSOR OF ANATOMY, HE STILL HAD NO IDEA
WHAT HAD HAPPEND TO HIM.
YES, IT WAS TRUE THAT THE SAC WAS EMPTY
NOW AND HIS OLD FAMILIARS WERE GONE,
BUT WHAT EXACTLY DID THAT MEAN?

THE JONESES HAD INTRODUCED HIM TO A DIFFERENT
WORLD FROM THE ONE HE HAD KNOWN WITH WILLY,
AND NOT A DAY WENT BY HE DIDN'T EXPERIENCE SOME
SUDDEN REVELATION OR FEEL SOME PANG ABOUT WHAT
HE HAD BEEN MISSING FROM HIS FORMER LIFE.

NOW THAT MR. BONES WAS ON THE INSIDE,
HE WONDERED WHERE HIS OLD MASTER HAD GONE
WRONG AND WHY HE HAD WORKED SO HARD TO
SPURN THE TRAPPINGS OF THE GOOD LIFE.

IT MIGHT NOT HAVE BEEN PERFECT
IN THIS PLACE, BUT IT HAD A LOT TO
RECOMMEND IT, AND ONCE YOU GOT USED
TO THE MECHANICS OF THE SYSTEM, IT NO
LONGER SEEMED SO IMPORTANT THAT YOU
WHERE TETHERED TO A WIRE ALL DAY.

TRAVEL WAS WHAT HE DID WITH WILLY,
AND IN ALL THE YEARS THEY HAD SPENT ON THE ROAD TOGETHER,
HE COULDN'T REMEMBER A SINGLE INSTANCE IN WHICH THE WORD
"VACATION" HAD CROSSED HIS MASTER'S LIPS.

TIME HAD FLOWED WITHOUT INTERRUPTION FOR THEM, AND
WITH NO NEED TO BREAK DOWN THE CALENDAR INTO
WORK PERIODS AND REST PERIODS, NO PARTICULAR
CALL TO OBSERVE NATIONAL HOLIDAYS, ANNIVERSARIES, OR
RELIGOUS FEAST DAYS, THEY HAD LIVED IN A WORLD APART,
FREE OF THE CLOCK-WATCHING AND HOUR-COUNTING
THAT TOOK UP SO MUCH OF EVERYONE'S ELSE'S TIME.

THE SYMPTOMS WERE STILL TOO VAGUE
TO PRODUCE ANY OUTWARD MANIFESTATIONS
(NO VOMITING, NO DIARRHEA, NO SEIZURES AS OF YET).
BUT AS THE DAYS WORE ON, MR. BONES FELT
LESS AND LESS LIKE HIMSELF, AND INSTEAD OF
TAKING THIS FAMILY VACATION BUSINESS IN HIS
STRIDE, HE BEGAN TO SULK AND BROOD ABOUT IT,
TO WORRY IT INTO A THOUSAND COMPONENT PARTS,
AND WHAT AT FIRST HAD SEEMED TO BE NO MORE
THAN A SMALL BUMP IN THE ROAD WAS TURNED
INTO A FULL-SCALE MISFORTUNE.

LONG

ILLY HAD NEVER LEFT HIM BEHIND.
NOT ONCE, NOT UNDER ANY CIRCUMSTANCES, AND HE WASN'T
USED TO THIS KIND OF HANDLING. PERHAPS HE HAD BEEN SPOILED,
BUT IN HIS BOOK THERE WAS MORE TO CANINE HAPPINESS THAN JUST
FEELING WANTED. YOU ALSO HAD TO FEEL NECESSARY.

DOG HAVEN WAS NO SING SING OR DEVIL'S ISLAND, NO INTERNMENT CAMP FOR ABUSED AND NEGLECTED ANIMALS. SITUATED ON A TWENTY-ACRE PROPERTY THAT HAD ONCE BEEN PART OF A LARGE TOBACCO PLANTATION, IT WAS A FOUR-STAR RURAL RETREAT, A CANINE HOTEL DESIGNED TO ACCOMMODATE THE NEEDS AND WHIMS OF THE MOST INDULGED AND DEMANDING PETS.

THEN THEY CLIMBED INTO THE VAN AND TOOK OFF, AND AS MR. BONES WATCHED THEM CHUG DOWN THE DIRT ROAD AND DISSAPEARS BEHIND THE MAIN HOUSE, HE HAD HIS FIRST INKLING OF THE KIND OF TROUBLE HE WAS IN.

IT WASN'T JUST A CASE OF THE BLUES, HE REALIZED, AND IT WASN'T JUST BECAUSE HE WAS SCARED. SOMETHING WAS SERIOUSLY WRONG WITH HIM, AND WHATEVER MAYHEM HAD BEEN BREWING IN HIM LATELY WAS ABOUT TO COME TO A FULL BOIL. HIS HEAD HURT, AND HIS BELLY WAS ON FIRE, AND A WEAKNESS HAD INVADED HIS KNEES THAT SUDDENLY MADE STANDING DIFFICULT

HE HAD SPENT TOO MUCH TIME FEELING
SORRY FOR HIMSELF LATELY, HAD FRITTERED
AWAY TOO MANY PRECIOUS HOURS POUTING
OVER INFINITESIMAL SLIGHTS AND INJUSTICES,
AND THAT KIND OF BEHAVIOR WAS UNSEEMLY
IN A DOG OF HIS STATURE.

THE MAN IN THE DREAM COULD HAVE BEEN
AN IMPOSTOR, A DEMON DRESSED IN WILLY'S FORM
WHO HAD BEEN SENT FROM TIMBUKTU TO TRICK
MR. BONES AND TURN HIM AGAINST HIS MASTER.
BUT EVEN IF IT HAD BEEN WILLY, AND EVEN IF
HIS REMARKS HAD BEEN STATED IN AN EXCESSIVELY
HURTFUL AND MEAN-SPIRITED WAY, MR. BONES
WAS HONEST ENOUGH TO ADMIT THAT THEY CONTAINED
A GERM OF TRUTH.

ENCOURAGED, HE FOLLOWED HER INTO THE HOUSE, THEN GRATEFULLY ACCEPTED HER OFFER TO LIE DOWN ON THE LIVING-ROOM RUG.

IT WASN'T THAT HE WAS IN TOP FORM, BUT AT LEAST HE WAS HALF ALIVE NOW, AND WITH HIS TEMPERATURE DOWN BY A COUPLE OF DEGREES, HE COULD MOVE HIS MUSCLES WITHOUT FEELING THAT HIS BODY WAS MADE OF BRICKS.

It made no difference to him whether he was sick or well, whether he was going to live or going to die. They had presented him with the last straw, and over his dead body would he ever allow them to take him to

THAT MORON OF A VET.

HE WENT AS FAR AS HIS LEGS COULD CARRY HIM, AND THEN, BETWEEN ONE STEP AND THE NEXT, WITHOUT THE SLIGHTEST PREMONITION OF WHAT WAS ABOUT TO HAPPEN, HE SANK TO THE GROUND AND FELL ASLEEP.

BONES KNEW WHERE HE WAS GOING, AND EVEN
E DIDN'T KNOW EXACTLY HOW TO GET THERE, HE
COUNTING ON HIS NOSE TO POINT HIM IN THE
T DIRECTION. THE JONESES' BACKYARD WAS ONLY
MILES AWAY, AND HE FIGURED HE WOULD ARRIVE
OMORROW, THE DAY AFTER THAT AT THE LATEST.
ER MIND THAT THE JONESES WERE GONE AND
LDN'T BE RETURNING FOR ANOTHER TWO WEEKS.

"What time, Willy?
What are you talking about?"
"When the time comes for you
to go to Timbuktu."
"You mean dogs are allowed?"
"Not all dogs. Just some.
Each case is handled separately."
"And I'm in?"
"You're in."

"Don't kid me, master.
If you're joking now,
I don't think I could stand it."
"Believe me, pooch, you're in.
The decision's been made."

"And when do I get to go?"
"When the time comes. You have to be patient."
"I have to kick the bucket first, don't I?"
"That's the deal. In the meantime, I want you
to be a good boy. Go back to Dog Haven and let
them take care of you. When the Joneses come
to pick you up, remember how lucky you've been."

Reluctant to leave the dream,
Mr. Bones only gradually became
aware of the intense cold around him,
and then, once he began to feel cold,
he became aware of an equally intense heat.

Something was burning inside him.

THE SUN WAS JUST COMING UP THEN, AND AS THE SNOW MELTED OFF THE TREES AND DROPPED TO THE GROUND IN FRONT OF HIM, MR. BONES WONDERED IF THE HIGHWAY WAS AS CLOSE AS IT SEEMED TO BE.

WILLY WOULD DISAPPROVE AT FIRST, BUT THAT WAS ONLY BECAUSE HE WOULD THINK THAT MR. BONES HAD GOTTEN THERE BY TAKING HIS OWN LIFE. BUT MR. BONES WASN'T PROPOSING ANYTHING AS VULGAR AS SUICIDE.

HE WAS MERELY GOING TO PLAY A GAME, THE KIND OF GAME THAT ANY SICK AND CRAZY OLD DOG WOULD PLAY. AND THAT'S WHAT HE WAS NOW, WASN'T IT?

A SICK AND CRAZY OLD DOG.

It was called dodge-the-car, and it was a venerable,
time-honored sport that allowed every old-timer to recapture
the glories of his youth. It was fun, it was invigorating,
it was a challenge to every dog's athletic skills.

Just run across the road and see if you could avoid being hit.
The more times you were able to do it, the greater the champion you
were. Sooner or later, of course, the odds were bound to catch up
with you, and few dogs had ever played dodge-the-car without losing
on their last turn.

But that was the beauty of this particular game.
The moment you lost, you won.

And so it happend, on that resplendent winter morning in Virginia,
that Mr. Bones, a.k.a. Spartakus, sidekick of the late poet Willy G.
Christmas, set out to prove that he was a champion among dogs.
Stepping off the grass on to the eastbound shoulder of the highway,
he waited for a break in the traffic, and then he began to run.

Weak as he was, there was still some spring left
in his legs, and once he hit his stride, he felt stronger
and happier than he had felt in months.

He ran toward the noise, toward the light, toward the glare
and the roar that were rushing in on him from all directions.

With any luck, he would be
with Willy before the day was out.